SOUTH SAN FRANCISCO PUBLIC LIBRARY

3 9048 02268723 4

W

S S.F. PUBLIC LIBRARY
WEST ORANGE

S S.F. PUBLIC LIBRARY
WEST ORANGE

SOUTH SAN FRANCISCO FREE PUBLIC LIBRARY

Records issued for 7 d
Overdue fine 5¢
Limit 6-LP rec
KEEP AWAY
BORROWER
CORD BEFORE
BORROWER MUST PAY FOR ALL
DAMAGE.
Thank you.

SEP 8 7

WE NEED TO DREAM
ALL THIS AGAIN

Plays by Bernard Pomerance

High in Vietnam, Hot Damn
Elephant Man

We Need to Dream All This Again

Bernard Pomerance

Viking

S.S.F. PUBLIC LIBRARY
WEST ORANGE

VIKING
Viking Penguin Inc., 40 West 23rd Street,
New York, New York 10010, U.S.A.
Penguin Books Ltd, Harmondsworth,
Middlesex, England
Penguin Books Australia Ltd, Ringwood,
Victoria, Australia
Penguin Books Canada Limited, 2801 John Street,
Markham, Ontario, Canada L3R 1B4
Penguin Books (N.Z.) Ltd, 182–190 Wairau Road,
Auckland 10, New Zealand

Copyright © Bernard Pomerance, 1987
All rights reserved

First published in 1987 by Viking Penguin Inc.
Published simultaneously in Canada

The epigraph is excerpted by permission from *Hamlin
Garland's Observations on the American Indian, 1895–1905*,
by Lonnie E. Underhill and Daniel F. Littlefield, Jr.,
Tucson: University of Arizona Press, copyright 1976.

Library of Congress Cataloging in Publication Data
Pomerance, Bernard.
We need to dream all this again.
1. Little Big Horn, Battle of the, 1876 — Poetry.
2. Custer, George Armstrong, 1839–1876 — Poetry.
3. Indians of North America — Wars — 1866–1895 — Poetry.
I. Title.
PR6066.048W4   1987   821'.914   86-40407
ISBN 0-670-81551-9

Printed in the United States of America
Set in Cochin
Book design by the Sarabande Press

Without limiting the rights under copyright reserved
above, no part of this publication may be
reproduced, stored in or introduced into a retrieval
system, or transmitted, in any form or by any means
(electronic, mechanical, photocopying, recording or
otherwise), without the prior written permission of
both the copyright owner and the above publisher of
this book.

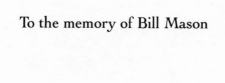

To the memory of Bill Mason

These lines are indebted to, I think at times in thrall to, the example of Christopher Logue's *War Music*. CL calls *War Music* an "account" of Books 16–19 of the *Iliad*. I would like these lines to be taken as an "account" of the last stage of the prolonged struggle between Lakota, Tsistsistas and Arapaho peoples on the one hand, and the U.S. government on the other, for the Black Hills.

There are many many sources and firsthand accounts of this period. That is history, it is called, and has its value. In sum I think it needs to be redreamed. Hence, the title. It is an experiment, an exercise. What it is not is history.

An old man raising the sun at dawn. A warrior-horse amalgam so well fitted as to reconstitute the centaur. These images, probably others, inspiration and friendship I owe Scott Momaday.

"Crazy Horse said to me, 'I'm glad you are come. We are going to fight the white man again.'

"The camp was already full of wounded men, women and children.

"I said to Crazy Horse, 'All right. I am ready to fight. I have fought already. My people have been killed, my horses stolen; I am satisfied to fight.'

"I believed at that time the Great Spirits had made Sioux, put them there . . . and white men and Cheyenne here . . . expecting them to fight. The Great Spirits I thought liked to see them fight; it was to them all the same like playing. So I thought then about fighting."

> — Two Moon, in an interview to
>   Hamlin Garland, 1898, from *Hamlin
>   Garland's Observations on the American
>   Indian 1895–1905*, (University of
>   Arizona Press, 1976)

PART ONE

The Words

SEDGWICK

1

Red Cloud's Vision:
The Word

What is the word?
The American assembly waits.

What is the word?
A breeze is bringing it.

The word is coming. The word is flying.
The word is running, jumping, gyring,
rising on a thermal, falling.

Eagle plumes fixed to lances, stir.
Eagle plumes float up from raven-colored hair;
now lift, now swing northwest.

Mahpiua Luta stands. Red Cloud stands. He combs the
breeze. It is the right word that he wants. He would use
millions if he knew it.

Or, *multitudes.*

"Locusts," he finally says. "They are like locusts."

The assembly listens. Lakota listen, also known as Sioux. some Tsistsistas too, also known as Cheyenne, murmuring, heads in rows like beads along the lines of abacus. Arapaho beside them listen too.

Two years from now Red Cloud will take a journey. Then he will see for sure. Mahpiua Luta will see Washington. He will be there. He will see as Chiefs before him have. As Chiefs before him he will see what his commander's eye must see; what when all is said and done, it was intended that he see: the numbers.

The numbers of the enemy.

"They are everywhere," he says. "Like locusts."

Red Cloud will see New York. In Washington, will be urged by officials: see New York. He will wish he was at home. Home, the interpreter will say. Chief Red Cloud would like to go home now. But: will be urged: go. Go present your case. Tell why the recent war. Explain the Powder River War. Tell why Oglalas fought. Why Lakota fought. Why U.S. soldiers died by Red Cloud's hand. Thus he will see New York. Will go from Washington by train. Will speak.

A huge indoor space. A stage. Gas lights. Cooper
Union Hall Presents. He will speak his case. The
Lakota case. The Oglalas case. The "Indian" case.
Will tell why he fought the Powder River War. Why
soldiers died. His interpreter will be faithful in the
manner of that year:

> "Chief Red Cloud says we fought
> because the government promised one
> thing and did another. They promised
> not to put any forts and soldiers on our
> hunting grounds. We knew what would
> happen, Chief Red Cloud says: buffalo
> be frightened, deer go away. We cannot
> eat then. We cannot live. Medicine
> creatures go, bear go, eagles go. Then
> too we cannot live. We said no to forts
> there. But secretly they put forts there,
> on that Bozeman trail. And soldiers
> same. And so we fought. We want
> promises kept. We want to live."

Silence. Mahpiua Luta will continue. The
interpreter:

> "Now those forts are gone. The
> government agreed. We never wanted
> to kill your soldiers; but now the
> government agreed. Now there can be
> peace. The Great White Father, Chief
> Red Cloud says, has promised that. He

has signed a Treaty. That is all we
wanted, Chief Red Cloud says. To be
living in our way as you live yours. He
has spoken."

Then New York will do something strange. Red
Cloud will be startled: by how suddenly they rise.
The strange crowd in that strange space in that city
New York. It will seem like fire starting on prairie
grass in summertime. You know how that rises
slowly at first. Just so, the audience; one man rising
first, two furious hands; then ten, then two, three,
four thousand hands crackling with applause.
Applause sweeping over all; applause filling in the
empty spots with surging noise like flames fill night
air; then like a skein of smoke rising thin at first,
drifting up above the flames, as the fire reaches
cottonwoods and pines at the forest edge, a lick
here, a crackle there, then roiling up in great
billows — just so this roar will billow up above the
applause.

Bravo, it will say. Bravo, Red Cloud.

Mahpiua Luta will know: it is a kind of love. But as
great speakers know, will know it is a love of —
theater; of good performance. Will know this love is
not enough. Will not firm up sovereignty. Will
wonder: Who else do they applaud? Do they
understand? About Indians? Treaties? Promises?
Peace? Their own government? What it does? Do
they grasp it?

A glance at the interpreter: *he*'s pleased. Red Cloud will accept it; must. But will also note again, will be unable not to see: the numbers. The numbers of the enemy.

This will happen two years from now.

Now, before the free assembled tribes, already he can make a practiced estimate by how many soldiers this government can lose, and not seem at all to count a grievous loss; and does: thus, to the people again:

> "Locusts," he says. "If —" expelling possibility, "it was a man — or just many men — I would say, I too am a man. We are many men. My heart grows angry and shouts to me, Fight them if they do me wrong!"

And pauses. He does not pause for effect. It is an obligation to be clear. It is his pride to be clear. He pauses to be clear. He, finally:

> "But they are not Shoshone. They are not Crow. They are not Pawnee. They are not like us . . . I do not think further war will get us something more. We have won a war. The forts are gone. I do not think we will win more. My heart then turns from war. My heart cannot feed orphans. It cannot repay those who lose a child in some future

war. We have won; we have strength
now. Now we can make peace from
strength, a good peace. There will be a
treaty council at Fort Laramie. I will
send someone to speak for me; I will
sign the treaty if it is what has been
promised."

People know: Red Cloud is right; Mahpiua Luta is
often right. He is right.

Now, another stands.

Since Time trudged out of caves, and with
bewildered blinks began to count the days and
nights, men have tried, not with much success, to
appear as this man does. Imagine an artillery shell,
impeccable in line, lifted from long ranks of
horizontal shells, mass rising slowly upright, to
vertical position. He has containment seemly to a
warrior. He has humility seemly to a medicine man.
Like that shell, he is powerful, contained,
mysterious, impossible to know completely and to
tell about it. Thus, Tatanka Iotanka stands, also
known as Sitting Bull.

His folded arms safety-pin a deerskin robe of star-
design about him, a bone horse-headed riding quirt
gripped in one fist.

Attention runs to him. He, to the point.

> "I do not wish to live on any
> reservation. That is what this treaty

means to me. I do not wish to have
some *wasichu* — meaning white man —
"tell me how to live, and where to live,
and who to worship, and what I am.
That is what this treaty means to me.
My father told me how to live. My
mother told me how to live. The
tunkashilas tell me how. The sky tells
me. The earth tells me. The winged
creatures tell me, the four-leggeds,
they tell me. Why do I need some treaty
to tell me. I do not need some treaty to
tell me. I do not wish some treaty to tell
me. I do not wish to lose by treaties
what I love. I do not wish treaties to
take something from me which I have
not lost. If I lose it, well then, it is
gone; but I have not lost it. I do not
wish to lose what was my father's, and
his father's, and given to the people by
the Creator and the *tunkashilas*. If
those grandfathers did not love us, how
would we have all this? If we do not
hold them, I do not think we will have
this. It is not mine to give away or
anyone's. If I would sign the treaty,
then, how would it be? Today, my
lands — gone. Tomorrow — the ways I
know are good — are gone. The next
day, or one more maybe — my eyes —
gone. They will dry up like leaves.
They will dry from seeing ruin. I will
see nothing then. That is how I think it

is with these treaty councils. Well, each
man must decide to go or not. Mahpiua
Luta wants to go. Then he must go.
Mahpiua Luta fought to save hunting
grounds he wanted. At Fort Laramie,
will he sign others' lands away? For
peace? I hope that he will not. I do not
know. I will not be there. He will not
sign for me. I cannot say we must make
peace while we have strength. I cannot
say we must move to reservations.
While we have strength — "

And nods now to his adopted younger brother Pizi,
also known as Gall — and more pointedly to Crazy
Horse, Tashunka Witko is his proper name, of Red
Cloud's own Oglalas, Tashunka Witko who has
helped Red Cloud whip Fetterman on the Powder,
and left 100 U.S. soldiers sprawled as carrion in
Montana —

" — it is, maybe, our last chance to use
it," Sitting Bull finishes. "I have
spoken."

And abruptly sits. His will radiates. And, he too is
right, the people know. And, too, has often been
right.

Red Cloud notes: he has not explained it well
enough. The numbers. The Enemy. He must rise
again; must balance arguments; must be clear about
the peril; must not arouse too great a sense of

futility; must not betray this free assembly to
despair. To be clear without being weak. He rises,
now confident.

He first recites his warrior's life. He unfolds his
success like a letter bearing good news. I will
remind you who I am. He reminds them who he is,
from the first Pawnee he killed, taking 21 ponies
swift and muscular, to the last *wasichu* in blue coat,
mustache, brass buttons, legs twisted under him,
flung down in the Powder River valley. His voice
begins to build. This is who I am. He is a
formidable speaker now, as in command of language
as he has been implicitly of men; and, as most pass
their lives with a wall between their thoughts and
their throats which their words cannot climb, but
fall back exhausted into dumbness and frustration,
Red Cloud's oratory has come to speak for them as
well. Now his voice comes in bursts of light and
dark, with shades of meaning no younger man, nor
any man will match today, nor often perhaps, ever.
He finishes:

> "If we are to fight, oh my brothers, *we
> are too few*. And if we are to die, *we
> are too many*. Yet — " not even glancing
> at, and not having to, Sitting Bull's
> Huncpapas, "each must decide for
> himself. I want peace now, a good
> peace which will last. A man from me
> will go to meet the Commissioners at
> Fort Laramie. I have spoken."

And abruptly sits. The line between Treaty faction
and anti-Treaty faction has been drawn. Later it will
read out as: Peace, War.

So it goes, each speaking in his turn (one with such
malevolence and mischief that no one can figure
which side he is on) until Tashunka Witko, Crazy
Horse:

> "You have said," to Red Cloud, "no
> white men in the Black Hills. Was that
> promised to you?"

But he does not say white men. He says, *wasichus*.
He does not say Black Hills. He says, *Paha Sapa*.
The Oglala says it gently — and yet, heads turn.
Eyes swivel round. Something stirs.

Crazy Horse is hard to pinpoint in an image, even
by Oglalas. Is he a great commander? Ask the
Crow, ask Shoshone. Great raider, horsethief? Yes,
all agree . . . But, as a man somewhat more solitary
than his success permits; somewhat more silent,
often seen afoot in his village head down in thought,
goshawk feather hanging, strolling, to disappear in
cottonwood groves. In what thought? No one can
say. Perhaps Ptehe Wohputa, Horn Chips, knows.
Horn Chips is a friend, a medicine man, a mentor,
he may have a clue.

Myself, I don't know much. I held a deerskin shirt
of his in my hands once. Its shoulders were a
powdery blue. It was so small and delicately made it

only added to the mystery. He was small; but did
not seem small. In war, was so volcanic, his
eruptions are used to date our strata still.

He was not known as a public speaker.

And perhaps the stir his words now cause is this: as
a man elusive, as a raider vivid, therefore by
extension when Tashunka Witko speaks, it creates
the seismics of a raid.

As for his mysticism, I imagine what is meant by
that, that bears speak in a vision, that skeins of
geese leave inter-agency memos scrawled on blue
Montana sky, that you may ride the horse of dreams
until you're in a lather, and the horse is still fresh,
ever-fresh, were only facts of life, which rested, and
still rest, as easily as this pollen-blue on his straight
Oglala shoulders.

Is this a raid? heads ask, glancing at Red Cloud.

It is Spotted Tail, a Brulé power allied to Red
Cloud, and Crazy Horse's uncle, who says:

> "It will be guaranteed. No white man in
> the Black Hills or any holy place or
> hunting ground."

Red Cloud, only then:

> "It was promised me."

Spotted Tail says:

"Unless we say we wish to sell them . . ."

Spotted Tail goes on, detailing possible conditions of
a land sale, Spotted Tail goes on about the number
of signatures which will be required to sell, Spotted
Tail goes on — and on — his intelligence and immense
command of detail now put shrewdly to this use: to
bore the more volatile hearts around his nephew
into numb responsibility. A final glance at Crazy
Horse. Sunken eyes gaze back, then down: at earth.

Red Cloud says:

"It was so. These things were
promised."

They wait. Earth rotates and puffs. Clouds scud. It
is still. Crazy Horse does not stand or speak or
move. He leaves respectful space between Red
Cloud's words and his own to come. Two
dragonflies hum left, then right.

The assembly waits.

In the left armpit of Crazy Horse, a small stone
vibrates. It is a small white stone, a *tunkan*, or spirit
stone, which has been neatly drilled through; it is
held in place by a buckskin thong. At times he feels
it vibrate.

This spirit stone was made for him by Horn Chips,
Ptehe Wohputa; it has protected him and helped

protect him in raids on Shoshone; raids on Crow; raids on U.S. soldiers. It has protected him from No Water, too.

When he took No Water's wife away, the wonderful Black Buffalo Woman, and when No Water came to Crazy Horse in revenge to blow his head off, and held the pistol out, and fired from not four feet away — well, that stone it is said, invested by Horn Chips with such power, this *tunkan*, it deflected No Water's bullet down, so that the Remington slug left only the slightest scar, a pale crescent beneath Crazy Horse's left nostril; not so much a scar these days as a sign of the divine protection Crazy Horse will bear as long as life bears him.

As Horn Chips murmurs now and then, Nothing in this word is real. The world of the spirits, the grandfathers, *tunkashilas*, that is real. Get your attention in that world, you will be invisible to harm in this one; this stone will help you, it will vibrate, you will have protection then — but, Tashunka Witko, listen: be careful: if you accept protection, you accept obligations. You must walk the sacred way. With the pipe must you walk. Not to, means death; or maybe something terrible . . . *Maka*'s flesh, you know . . . Earth's flesh is yours; *skan*'s breath, your breath. If you accept protection, do not fail Earth your mother when she needs your shield. Be of the same mind as her. Never pretend you don't know her. Now we will smoke, we will pray her help.

Rising now, finally, Crazy Horse goes not left or
right, but — imagine Dr. J. driving on Bill Russell —
takes it straight to Red Cloud. Thus:

> "Another treaty? . . . another?" Pause.
> "But I . . . would be ashamed before my
> father," pointing out the older Crazy
> Horse by chin nod, "to give more
> sacred earth for another treaty,
> meaning nothing. For I do not know
> what any treaty got the Lakota from
> them" — meaning whites — "except
> grief." Pause. "Unless you count their
> arrogance."

His father stares into the ground. Horn Chips
blinks. The course is clear to all now. Crazy Horse:

> "The Lakota had a treaty . . ." His
> voice, slow, soft, brings heads forth to
> hear him. "It said, No forts. But, forts
> were built; on our hunting grounds.
> Soldiers came. We had to fight. And we
> drove them out, and punished them.
> And now: they want — another
> treaty . . .

> "Another . . . 'to last forever' . . . Well, I
> wonder. When an Indian does not fight,
> I don't think they say, That Indian is
> fair; he loves peace and the Great Spirit
> like we do." Thinks. "They say: That

Indian is weak. Kill him. He is a dog.
Beat him. He is a fool — fool him.

"To sign another treaty won't bring
Lakota peace. It will only make us seem
weak and stupid. Then why should
they leave us anything? Who sees they
love us? I only see they hate us. Even
so . . ." now thinking out loud, ". . . even
so . . ." the sign of a bad speaker, but
for a moment drinking in the air so
filled with cedar, pine and spruce his
lungs feel punched out by sheer
greenness, "The Creator made them too
. . . If they are fools, it is not for me to
say so. Or to hate. But, reservations . . .
no. I am Lakota. I do not wish to live
on one. I do not wish to be a worthless
drunken man. I prefer this life we have.
If I sign this treaty, how will I hunt? I
know how: with their permission; when
they give it. But I am permitted by my
Creator . . . I do not need any other
permission.

"And the Black Hills . . . well, how is it
truly with their promises?" Head
lowered; terminal thoughtfulness; head
up, sunken eyes again: "Locusts," to
Red Cloud. "You have said, Locusts.
My heart says: Yes, and their promises
are Locusts' promises. When they are

17

hungry, treaty or no treaty, they will
rise, like a dark cloud, and be between
us and the sun. And they will eat.

"I will not sign. I have spoken."

And, sits. Red Cloud, angry, dismayed, does not
move. Horn Chips, Ptehe Wohputa thinks: will eat
and strip every tree, even the sacred tree of life;
even of every leaf; of our lives.

It is Spotted Tail quick to rise, so graceful you do
not note his haste, but speed a clue to the suddenly
alarmed communal sense: collision between two
powerful Oglalas, it would be dangerous now, must
be averted, no time to waste.

Spotted Tail, thus to his feet, quickly slips in;

> "Each must decide for himself to attend
> Fort Laramie or not, and to sign the
> Treaty or not to. Before deciding that,
> must consult and talk, and hear
> everything that is being offered. Well,
> there is time enough for that. I say that
> is what we must do now."

And to underline communal alarm, let Crow Dog
rise here too. Crow Dog lost his wife to Spotted
Tail; Spotted Tail just stole her. He feels stabbed
each time he sees the man. He shows nothing of it.
Instead he pulls his chin, squints and looks around,

and thinks: bad enough this snake turd took her; worse for anyone to think I care; worst of all in times like these to show personal spite, and be thought selfish. He is not selfish. Ten, twelve years from now, having nursed his aggravation through war, defeat and other hardship, he will walk calmly into Spotted Tail's tipi, and shoot him dead, and no one call him selfish then. But that is years from now. Now he rises in aid of the community, to surprisingly say:

"I agree with that man."

And sits. And radiates his will.

The meeting slowly breaks. They have heard. War and Peace, Treaty-yes and Treaty-no, have certain common needs. They have immediate needs. One, to think. Two, to piss. They think. They piss. They shake. They think.

Red Cloud thinks: I did not tell them what I know, not well enough. The numbers. The numbers of the enemy. He is not used to failure. He is tired. He blots the meeting out. He has spoken. The confusion of the world has garbled his intention.

Sitting Bull thinks: he must hold the next sundance. He must pray unceasingly for power; must guide adopted younger brother Gall towards all the ancient wisdoms he can bear; towards a single point: Save us, or we lose all.

Chief Gall, exceptional Huncpapa warchief, orphaned by white soldiers, glances at his Oglala counterpart, Crazy Horse. Eyes meet. Crazy Horse sees war in Gall's. Gall sees death. Ah. More desolate than he remembered. Tashunka Witko's eyes show nothingness. He is there. Yet he is not. It is powerful. Two black eye-magnets hold the iron in Gall fast. A magpie darts between the Chiefs. Gall shakes his glance away, forgets what he has seen.

The magpie takes the memory for its nest.

Crazy Horse, abruptly business-like, takes aside another man: this one is squat and powerful, badger-like, you would not like to be wriggling in his jaws. He inclines his head to hear the voice. His name is Little Big Man. Crazy Horse says, "I will not go to Fort Laramie. I will not sign the treaty. I wish for you to go there for me. Say this to any Chief who signs . . ." And tells him.

Ptehe Wohputa, Horn Chips, watches from a distance. His eyes are gentle and extremely clear, and there is that attentiveness about his being that you often find in people who see what others do not. He sees not two men talking, but one man turning another into a weapon.

If Sam Colt had been commissioned to make the perfect pistol for Tashunka Witko and Colt had said, Sure, okay, how'd Crazy Horse like it? Barrel? Adornment? Single or double? And then Colt had been told: make it single action, barrel not too long, five inches say, but good stopping power, .44 will do, and Colt had set his Hartford workshop working, and had produced this thing of hard and shining steel and engraved the pistol with hunting scenes both delicate and strong, you know, dogs apoint, a pheasant flushed, a male deer between two firs, and then that splendid weapon were to be transformed into a man, that man might be something like Little Big Man.

His eyes soften as Crazy Horse speaks, from obsidian to soft tar. He nods. He nods. He will do as asked. He goes; Little Big Man goes.

A seven-foot-tall Cheyenne who has been waiting now approaches. When this solemn man rises from the ground after any council, he is a wonderment. His name is Face in Clouds Speaking.

Not even in reservation days to come will anyone dare confront this man with the Bering Strait Migration Theory (being popularized this instant to undermine his rights of tenure). He comes from the Buffalo People. They came from the Earth. That is all there is to it. And it is so. See him walk. Earth-colored and stupendous, his shoulders nudge ancestral buffalo aside. His face is painted black. An outlined bolt of lightning streaks from lower eyelids down each cheek. Across broad lips, an outlined human hand in white, signaling feat of hand-to-hand combat; six eagle feathers fanned out flat along unbraided raven hair semaphore: other coups, other coups. As he halts before Crazy Horse, his placid eyes show great alarm. His lips stay sealed: for Face in Clouds Speaking is a tongue-tied man. Only in song does his speech impediment dissolve. But his hands can, do speak.

They are immense and wide and knobbly. He is left-handed, too. Now sign language flies off his fingers like whorls off a stenographer. His breath, short, frustrated bursts, Buffalo breath.

His hands dictate to Crazy Horse: I have two wives. I hear about reservations, they will make me choose. They are sisters. I love them both. They belong together. If I choose one, I would not blame the other if she poisons me. How can I separate them? I cannot. It is wrong. It is wrong. What you said I say too: I will not go to the treaty council. I will not touch the pen. Your wife is Cheyenne: you understand. We Cheyenne call you brother. Brother! God gave me no words. That great truth I am denied. But one truth he gave me: behold me as I am. Brother! if you fight I will be there. Brother! even if it is you alone to fight, you will not be alone. On your left will I be; and on my left — Death. Brother, we will be there. I have spoken.

His pent-up message delivered, glad, Face in Clouds Speaking turns and ambles back to Two Moon's camp, hands silent at his flanks. At camp, dogs go mad around his knees. He cuffs two, kicks one away, one picks up, rubs its nose, bends, enters tipi, backhands dog out, smiles at his two treasures; one feeds an infant, one pointedly ignores him. Ah, they are beautiful, no women like the Cheyenne, they are the Pleiades . . . Except maybe for the gossip . . . Life is good.

Outside, Moon glides up the sky.

It is 1868. The Fort Laramie Treaty is signed that year; but not by all. The Black Hills are reserved to Indian use and occupation; they are acknowledged as a sacred ground.

Six years later, in the Black Hills gold is found.

2

The Black Hills:
God Without Humanity

Someone said some time ago: the desert is just God
without humanity.

He could have said the Black Hills. The Paha Sapa.

These hills make bumps, outcroppings of stone
fringed by pines, an outbreak of fantastic symptoms
of mountains to come further west.

Clouds have crashed and turned to rocks.

The Black Hills lie at the crossroads where
Wyoming, Montana and South Dakota,
unemployed, all hang around a corner. Geological
death is here.

Something that has lasted beyond death is here.
Spirit is here. Death far greater in scale than our
own is here. A vast mimicking of immortality.

Perhaps that is why you can see that they are holy.
The place is holy. Visions can be cried for here.
Here a bear might speak to you; a line of ants; a
wolf look up suddenly; an otter tell all you need to
know; a spider too, perhaps. Perhaps that is why
you can see that they are sacred. Perhaps it is what
sacred means, what holy means: that which imitates
that which does not vanish.

They will never vanish, never. They are sacred. Or,
so Lakota say. So Tsistsistas say.

What do the goldminers say? Now miners pour into
the Black Hills. What do they say about it?
Specifically, what do they say about death and
immortality, and the sacred, what is the vision they
seek here?

The miners have a joke: Gold is just god with an
'l,' bub.

They begin to find it, too.

Eureka.

3

The Assembled Generals:
The Word

Before the assembled Generals, Colonel Custer
finds the word he's looking for.

> "Millions," he says.

In gold.

> "California," he says. "It will be
> California all over again."

California! Still a magic word. The golden state.

> "As for keeping the white man out . . ."
> Custer does not ruminate, but likes
> suspense: "*No.* There will be no way.
> There is gold there. White men will go.
> The Black Hills must be open to them,
> treaty or no treaty."

Shaking his shoulder-length golden locks, Custer finds his eloquence; after all, who are these miners? General Sheridan nods: good question, who. Smiles at Custer, encouraging the revelation, which Custer makes, forefinger stabbing palm: *They are men!*

Oh. Heavy-lidded, General of the Armies Sherman leans, whoops an oyster-like object plop into a spittoon.

Men, Custer continues, or the descendants of men who came to America to get rich. That is who the miners are.

How "nice" are they? Who cares? Custer? He allows just how damn nice they are. For they say they came to America to be free. By free, of course they meant rich. But they did say free, and what more can you ask. The verbal good manners of America make any man nice. Cortez . . . Cortez led the way, or Columbus if you wish. Be damned sure they didn't fry old Montezuma's feet just to be free. Gold is not a metal, gentlemen. It is the promise of the continent. I ask you to imagine some dirty cooper outside Akron, six grubby kids banging at his knees. Keep that man from the Black Hills? Forget it. That man *is* Cortez.

Some thoughts that scoot around the polished walnut conference table: *Already?* Custer's rehearsing campaign speeches already? He aims to be President one day, that's pretty clear — but —

good God — *dirty cooper? grubby kids?* The tone is
wrong. It is incompetent, fearless, arrogant. Not
unlike the man himself.

A one-armed General feels a prickling at his lips,
thinks, Got to get this beard trimmed.

> "Gentlemen," Custer says, "we have
> already made a solemn commitment to
> the American people. When we back
> the transcontinental railroads, for
> example." This, a nice dig at the Boss;
> General of the Armies Sherman's old
> Engineering Corps pals built the
> railroads with full Army protection.
> "When we exterminate the Buffalo to
> starve out a way of life, we, I say, have
> made a commitment. I refer to our
> civilizing mission on this continent.
> Gentlemen! Treaty or no treaty, with
> that mission foremost in our minds, we
> cannot hesitate to protect our miners in
> the Black Hills. If the Sioux reject the
> mission destiny puts before us, we must
> act decisively."

General of the Armies Sherman thinks: Oh hell, just
ten a.m. and the shit's already reached my ankles.
And he tunes out.

> *Of all the Generals present,*
> *Sherman must be foremost.*
> *This story is told and it is true,*

tho I'll improvise here just a bit:
In the recent War Between the States
when Sherman lit his Armies up
like a terrible match ten miles long
and dragged its blaze through Georgia
west to east
he conceived a terrible passion:
begged permission from shocked Grant
to acetylene his way northwards,
barbecue both Carolinas
reach Richmond grim as Nemesis —
stalking out of a column of smoke —
and for a grand finale
whack his phosphorous head
smack against Virginia and go
Whoosh!

Grant ordered Sherman home by sea.
A sea cure for a war-sick man?
The Atlantic being fireproof, he
glared at the waves reproachfully
and tossed cigar butts in.

"Protection for the miners," Custer
concludes his show-and-tell, "will be an
Army matter."

A General with one arm who shall be nameless:

"George, we all know you're the one
who started this gold rush — Oh yes
you did, George, and we know it. You
surveyed the Black Hills, found gold,

ran off to the goddamned New York
papers; you got the story spread. You
started it. Now, *Colonel*—"

Call Custer *Dog* instead! How he hates the word
Colonel. A field commission Major General in the
war; returned to Colonel in postwar rank
allotments, he freezes at the sound of it.

The one-arm:	"*Colonel*, if that wasn't exceeding your functions as an officer of the United States Army, I don't know what is. You encourage fellow citizens to head for the Black Hills; which you know is to violate a solemn Federal treaty with the Sioux and Cheyenne tribes. Now, with your customary gall you want to shoot the Army in to protect men who oughtn't to be there in the first place. Well—I have little doubt there *will* be trouble; and we *will* be called upon to move troops in, in further violation of that treaty. I am frankly wondering if we shouldn't stop it now."
Custer, ice cream:	"Why, I thought you had a question at first. I'm not sure I understand."
The General:	"Yes I have a goddamned question! What the hell are you up to? I say if we go in, we go pull the miners out right now!"

Phil Sheridan, who promotes Custer, who has New
York friends Sheridan would dearly like:

> "Let's not overstate that problem . . . I
> think the Colonel's covered all that . . ."

The one-arm:

> "Why no he hasn't — George's contempt
> is so big he hasn't even bothered to
> cover his goddamned ass. All *he's* going
> to cover is cover us all with dishonor,
> totally, totally, as bullies, liars and
> treaty breakers."

Sheridan:

> "Now, we'll be negotiating to buy those
> Black Hills from the Sioux, and while
> we do, what harm is there —"

And one-arm:

> "The Sioux won't sell a sacred place!
> That's all horse-pucky!" And clamps
> his lips.

Custer, bathing in the attention, to General of the
Armies Sherman:

> "Sir, at the risk of being obvious, you
> will need commanders who know both
> the Plains and the Indians."

Now the one-armed General who shall be nameless
did not mean to speak again. He understood the

flow of opinion in the room, and wished to stay just discreet enough to influence events in the future. It was just unfortunate for him that a ghost was in the room.

She was a woman once, Cheyenne, nobody very special, except perhaps in her own village, an encampment on the Washita, where her quillwork was thought matchless. She had the sharpest eyes, the deftest fingers you can imagine. She has followed Custer near ten years, trying to get his attention. It began when one of his horsetroopers, not comprehending Cheyenne or not caring, ignoring her upraised arms as she kept mouthing, Good Indian, no, Good Indian, whacked his saber down on the soft part where the shoulder joins the neck, generally a graceful line you may notice when a woman smiles, cutting a number of her lifelines and she fell. It was one of those embarrassing massacres: the Cheyenne village was flying the American flag when attacked. Since then, she has tried everything to get the Commander's attention. She pulls his hair. She howls the "Garry Owen" in his ear at night. When he's in the midst of trying to give that Libby a good one, she bends his cock in half. Nothing seems to work. He does not seem to notice. It is just as bad as life was.

Now she sees her chance. She pries open the grimly set white beard and teeth of the one-armed General — his eyes widen in angry surprise — and hops right up on his tongue, and murmurs to everyone's affront:

"By commanders who know the Plains
and Indians, the dickhead maybe means
those who've slaughtered them
indiscriminately?"

Oh Lord, oh my. See Sherman glare at that one.
General Sheridan, as if a bad odor had wafted in
the tall-windowed room:

"Oh, come on, Otis, will you? . . ."

Military hrumphs and grumbles:

"Past is past . . . stop farting around . . .
best of us makes mistakes sometimes . . ."

Custer, coolly:

"Wait — no, wait. General —" to the
one-arm. "No man stands before me in
his admiration of the Plains Indians
way of life. Why I find it enviable. You
may read that in my memoirs, sir. The
Freedom. The Warrior's way, the
hunting life; and dare I say, the
women's warmth and: honesty — why, if
I were one of them, I would never give
it up. For what? Whiskey? Idleness?
Not on your life, I'd rather die. But I
am not one of them. Like you, I am one
of the White Race. Greater things are
expected of us, don't you think? I
sure do."

Sheridan: "Well put, George."

Dear God! Sherman thinks. The shit has reached
my knees . . . !

But it is clear to all now: the amounts of gold are
staggering. The pressure from Congress, a body
never known to be immune to the love of gold, and
in this, Grant's second administration, a body
ravaged by its utter lack of that immunity, pressure
from that haggard entity will build till it is
staggering. Troops will be called for to protect the
miners, treaty or no treaty. The Fort Laramie Treaty
is staggering. All is staggering.

Dare we pile on a messenger?

Enter a messenger.

He extends a telegram. Sherman glares the glare he
glares when he wants to be read to. The aide reads:

             "Two miners . . . killed . . . Black Hills
             . . . Indian Agent hysterical. . ."

Two. Two killed. Custer sighs ostentatiously, and
shakes his lowered head. A sign, this shake says. He
knew it would happen in this way.

Sheridan, nursing the telegram:

"Damnation . . . outrageous . . ." and
looks to Sherman.

Sherman, warrior sick of Washington, sick of desks,
offices, ambitious subordinates, sick of dumb-ass
conferences, sick of Custer, who half-consciously he
identifies with Indians in that the only good Custer
would be a dead one; Sherman hoods his violent
eyes, rehearses what he'll say to the President, who,
leaving office in disgrace soon, will not care much
now one way or another what anyone says to him:
and shrugs assent:

"Okay. If it's begun, we'll finish it."

And will order Armies of the west to converge,
Crook's and Terry's, yes, and to force the last Sioux
and Cheyenne onto reservations; or to crush them
once and for all.

It is night. The Cheyenne ghost goes to the Eastern
shore. She prays for dawn to come. She will ride an
ultraviolet ray home. Reft of longing, home still
means something, tho what is hard to say. I would
not mind to be, she thinks, a sparkle on a ripple at
that blue bend of the Washita. I am ready, thinks
the ghost, I guess . . . Now let me be light.

In the Black Hills, Crazy Horse enters the fourth
night of his fasting. Tears pouring out, he cries for
pity from the Creator. He cries to live in harmony
with all his relations, with all that is sacred. He cries

for a vision to shore him up for what he's sure will
come. Exhausted, he ceases. He waits. A breeze
posts up, fakes, double-fakes, drives the lane
between tobacco offerings and leaps. He starts
again.

Some miles away on the plain, Horn Chips sits in a
circle of men. He stares ahead, listens, attentive. At
Crazy Horse's own request he has put him on the
hill again. It is the *yuwipi* man's fourth night at
ground control. The night is crickety. He listens.
Now, frogs. He listens. Is it — ? The approach — ?
He listens. Silence. Void. Silence? Where are the
crickets? The frogs? . . . Then, sparks prance in the
dark.

He unwraps pipe. he unwraps stem. No waste
motion, fits stem to pipe, fills bowl, feels the power
flow from this completed circuitry, lights sacred
pipe, and powerfully, to Wakantanka and to the
West, Horn Chips begins to chant. The men
respond, *Hau!* Powerfully to the North he chants.
The men respond. Powerfully to the East he chants.
The men respond. To the South he chants. The men
respond. To the Above he chants. The men respond.
To the Below he chants. He chants powerfully. The
men respond. To the Spotted Eagle, prayer carrier,
he chants. Powerfully he chants. The men respond.

We want safety for that man on the hill!
The men respond.

He wants to live in harmony with all his relations!
The men respond.

He cries to you for help. He cries to you for a vision
to guide him. That is why we cry to you. Accept
this smoke. Accept our breath. Accept these
offerings and pity us.

Horn Chips lays out the skin offerings.

The men say: Pity us! Let us live!

4

Hey, American Light,
This Bud's for You:
June 1, 1876

Night
and Ocean sway apart, upper
and lower eyelids.
Light spills first on Washington.

         No breeze today.

White glares off white.

         Air heavy; haze, a marble monument.

Humid blossoms stare at earth.

         Ritual prostitutes perform in congress,
         sweaty, tranced; now wipe brows,
         now cry out.

White House spittoons fill up.

> On the bridle path in the park,
> prosperous thief tips hat to
> prosperous thief: "Hot enough
> for you today? . . ." "Sir . . ." They pass.

A white-bellied goat —
for accounting purposes, called a Secretary —
is prepared for sacrifice.
Her pale throat beats.

> Her boss, malfeasant, watches.
> This ritual will atone him if . . .
> she'll only keep her mouth shut.
> Ah that mouth . . . He sweats. She
> clears her desk.

The Imperial City sweats.

> Mist struggles off Potomac swamps;
> burst possum corpse exhales . . .

In the War Department an aide
to General of the Armies Sherman
shuts the thick green velvet drapes:
not to keep light out, but the Chief's
fearful stare within. Scrutinizing
documents, the great soldier's radar
eyes sweep left, sweep right:

Fort Laramie Treaty . . . blip . . .
Fetterman massacre . . . blip . . . *Reynolds*
says Crazy Horse . . . blip . . . *Crazy*
Horse, Oglala Sioux Chief . . . blip . . .
blip . . . *Black Hills*, blip, *gold*,
blip . . . *Sitting Bull hostile* . . . *Sitting*
Bu —

"Bullshit!" Sherman slams
his desk. "Open the goddamned drapes!"

Light sprints off the starting blocks,
hurdles West Virginia, stride,
hurdles Pennsylvania, stride, now hurtles west express
no local stops.

        Light clears Ohio now, coursing
        the ancient river bed

Light tucks one arm behind
speedskates Indiana haze

        Light longjumps Illinois, ties
        its world mark for the span,

Light wears the dawn team colors,
hop-step-leaps the Mississippi! —

        plows into Iowa, is up and flying,
        flying,

fans Nebraska, both Dakotas flat
with flaming heat

and
still striding easily,
now slanting left for balance,

rounds the curve of Earth, and — go! —

now pours it on
towards Crazy Horse,
Tashunka Witko praying,
on a hilltop in Montana,
arms flung Eastward,
pipe held out,
head flung back crying,
crying,

Tunkashila Wakantanka!
Tunkashila Wakantanka!
Tunkashila Wakantanka!
Tunkashila Wakantanka!

Wakantanka
        umshimala ye!
Wakantanka
        umshimala ye!
Mitak' uye
        ob wani kta
ca lecamun welo!

Fat profiteroles
of chubby cloud now swiftly part
before

                  — ca lecamun welo! —

             The Presence

humped
upon light's back.

PART TWO

Black Hills
Hallucinations

1

Tashunka Witko a/k/a
Crazy Horse Prays at Dawn

From this mountainous cloud
dear God — see?
that praying speck.

> Down — there —
> follow my finger — there.
> That dot with knees and pleas.

Going on four days like that.

> God sees.

His radiant hands
light-bearing filaments
fan out. Wide. Now, wider.

Now, He flexes knees. Tests
perfect balance on tiptoe —

now, bounce — jump! —
airborne! —
double backflip, two twists and a half,
triple pike, finishing tuck — ah,
terrific. The six grandfather judges
give Him perfect scores for entry.

Like eagle down
Dawn
touches earth.
He crouches in the dust:

"Tashunka Witko . . ." *Crazy Horse.*
Words, like humming wings.

Crickets quit.
Near-ripe cherries ripen —
pop! — orgasmically.
That's the way it is these visits.
Things are overdone, perhaps . . . but,
alas — not perfect. Look:

A female hump of rodent fur
wrapped round a tiny heart
prays at an upraised grain — industriously! —
oblivious her fate breathes near.

So! God thinks, knowing in advance.
And, turns back to the praying man.

The mortal, still. Another pebble; gravel
among gravel pebbles in the sun.
His heart beats through his back.

"Psst: Crazy Horse . . ." Waits.
"Listen to Me carefully." One strategist
to another: "If, that is," dangling the
carrot now, "you mean to save
the Black Hills." *From wasichus* . . .

The two-legged, shut-eyed, sweats.

"The —" in perfect Lakota now,
"Paha Sapa." Speaking 4000
tongues like a native, as they say:
shifts again mysteriously: *from white men.*

Finally, one General to another:
"I will send you strategy by Dreams Express.
Pay attention and you will win . . ."
Almost adds, but doesn't: "For a while . . ."

> Behind shut lids, Tashunka Witko
> now attends — what's this? —
> beating wings, dragonflies,
> four wings humming, dancing
> somehow like the voice of June.

> It sounds to him like this:
> Nothing on this earth is real,
> Tashunka Witko. Nothing.

> His eyes slide open. All
> the way down the long Montana sky,
> swimming, a V of geese.
> Suddenly, swerves East.

Soldiers. From the Southwest,
from the East. Coming soon.
He knew anyway . . . still . . .
every little bit of help will help.

> Tuck, triple pike, two twists
> and a half,
> double backflip back-
> wards, God runs his own
> film in reverse,
> hops back to heaven,
> smiles and stretches, left-
> handed flicks
> a spotted hawk down on the mouse.

> Says, "I will flood the earth this
> week —"

waits for protests —
there are none —
suddenly grins — those wonderful teeth!
(tho some think the canines a bit long)

> " — with dreams."
> He looks around. "I
> feel good . . . I FEEL GOOD!"

Below the cherries plop to earth.
The mouse is ripped.

2
Sherman Scares a Map

In Washington
General of the Armies
William Tecumseh Sherman
scares the shit out of a map
just by glaring at it.

Up it snaps, back on-
to its roller.
He draws it firmly down again.

The Department of the Missouri.
In the middle of the continent,
an uncivilized middle name.
Like his own, Tecumseh, Indian.

Tecumseh — launched a thousand
schoolyard fights? Two thou?
Now recalls the first boy,

bashed face down, repenting bloody
mouth in dirt, Sherman's fist up to
strike again, again: *Not Tecumseh — Bill,*
Bill, Bill, Bill! Boy shrieks: *Bill!*
And found he had a taste for
countrymen crying mercy and his name . . .

> If names had throats — !
> *I'd strangle it . . .*

Suddenly, all goes dark. Oh God! Again!
His eyes pop out, bounce away like
tennis balls. A bland aide at his side,
reminds. Oh yes . . . They'll be back.
"Just at the photographer's . . ."
His famous glare's in such demand
it sits for portraits in his stead.

Blind power waits for news.

> The Imperial City waits.

3

The Dream-like Countdown

Dreams Express delivers.
Tashunka Witko dreams the clue:

>Two spears
>here — you see? and here.
>
>Blade beside blade, shafts twinned,
>parallel. *Like closed scissors.*
>Markings, Lakota and Shyela.
>
>Thrust them together. Then withdraw,
>Tashunka Witko.
>Draw back.
>Divide them like a gesture of welcome,
>Tashunka Witko. *Open scissors wide.*
>When they charge in, as, oh yes,
>they will charge in,
>rotate the shafts around

their wider axes—
swerve warponies around, thus,
left and right—got that?—
bite the blades back inwards then,
snip the American flanks
here—thus—and, thus—here.

· · ·

They see the runner first,
the women picking berries.

Feet flying, hair flying back,
he closes on the Indian village.

> *Seen from above, 3000 tipis,*
> *a yellow crescent moon*
> *curved to a reclining hip*
> *of the Rosebud River banks.*
> *A scurrying ant.*

One points him out. She,
the wife of Wooden Leg, who
can run a deer to breathlessness.
The women do not speak. In the
runner's mouth, they know,
carried deferentially as a kitten:
Soldiers coming—soon.

> Nimble fingers hasten.
> Berries pile quickly up,
> tiny heads. A child's mouth,
> smudged red, fingers juicy.

As two swallows dart to nest at dusk,
just so the runner's legs
fly into the village.

          .   .   .

Tatanka Iotanka too dreams,
a/k/a Sitting Bull,
dreams soldiers falling from on high
hail-like
spurting hot red soup
from severed necks
into an Indian camp.

Sitting B. next day at *inipi*
gesturing incisively with a
sprig of sacred sage
through sweatlodge steam
believes the signs are good.

It looks all systems go.

                    Trailing steam now
they emerge,
the holy men, the warriors,
purified,
ready for the paint.

Hear how they leave the Sweat
behind:

Sitting Bull, emerging,
gravely: *Mitak' oyassin.*

Now, emerging, straightening up,
Hump: *Mitak' oyassin.*
Now, Gall: . . . *oyassin.*
Now Horn Chips: . . . *oyassin.*
Now Crazy Horse: . . . *oyassin.*
Now Two Moon of the Cheyenne,
now Dull Knife: *Mitak' oyassin!*
Now Iron Thunder: . . . *oyassin.*
Lame Deer: . . . *oyassin!*
Yellow Hand,
Spotted Tail: . . . *oyassin! oyassin!*

Mitak' oyassin: All are Relatives.

Grave. Purified. Ready
for the paint.

A people who conceive themselves as great
for being relatives of everything
and see their blessings everywhere
don't like to imagine the Unfair has
their number, too. It is: inconceivable . . .
Thus now they do not deign to speak
of Paha Sapa, the Black Hills;
of railroads wooing landscape through
piled-high bone ricks, hides and tongues
of the deconstructed buffalo —
the sun's nuncio on earth —
nor of goldminers and pickaxes

thudding at the navel of the world
nor of wasichu insults, nor
treaties made in good faith shattered,
nor even of Sherman's armies coming
to convert these crimes to martial law.
Being unfair thus, it is . . . inconceivable.

And they do not need to speak.

One shaman lights the cedar chips.
He waits; his eagle-wing fan waits.
His importance becomes a trance.
Man with fan becomes eagle now,
wonderful, precise,
murmurs and waves cedar smoke
where it must do its good.

Sitting B., facing his
adopted nephew/younger brother
Pizi, also known as Gall:

The paintpot waits.

The older chief, face intent.
Imagine a bird of prey
up on a thermal. He
knows ripeness more acutely
than the hummingbird.

A whole horse nation waits.

No warning—all is ripe.
Abrupt, Sitting B. bends, dips fingers,

drags the first white stripe of
paint from Gall's left cheek
up across that nose
to Gall's right cheek.

Eye catches eye.

Uncle passes black-hole
gravity to nephew. In
that instant, Gall knows,
and we do,
what war for the holy
Black Hills means.

Wipe-fade one moment
to the distance
to a glossy postcard
of the Bighorn Mountains saying Cheese,
a meadow in the foreground
so green and so alive
it must be tentpegged to the hillside
by 484 tall pines, or it would
rise and flap and glide around:
a spotted pony there, well
prepared for war,
veteran nose stooped to sweetgrass,
chewing,
chewing —
stops.

Looks up.

Shiny brown eye,
mirror of his master's.

Nose up, ears up, then

He stamps the earth,
prances left
He stamps the earth now
prances right,
He stamps the earth,
prances forward,
He stamps the earth,
prances backward,
head tossed to clouds,
now snorts down,
He prances all directions,
stops —

                    He also shits. That too,
                    part of it.

He stills sleek muscles
suddenly

Listens

Nostrils beating
like fool hearts —

to the countdown
no one else can hear.

Interlude: The Sleep of the Warshields

They sleep like racks of batteries in rows
in some shut-down garage at night.

On circular wooden rims, rounded
buffalo hide stretched dry, the
Sioux warshields.

Painted on this disk, the
trademark: flying things.
This, the sleeper's medicine:
the butterfly, and crow,
the hawk and dragonfly,
magpie with striped wing,
bat with red eyes, swallow, goose;
big-shouldered in the center,
the messenger from above:
Eagle.
Lightning zooms down off his wings.

From this, an otter tail hangs.
From that, a wolf's. There
eagle plumes surround the rim,
an eclipsed sun's penumbra,
the quills precision-engineered
to fold down corps-de-ballet-like
inside the shield's case.

Painted on this disk: two bears,
stretched vermilion bears
at the shield's top and bottom arcs,
archaic and ancestral bears,
white breathlines arcing down
into the solitude of Grizzly hearts.
One megaton apiece, they
stalk around infinity. In the
hub, a four-clawed paw upraised:
Halt! Power at Work Here.

                    Painted on each shield,
                    Medicine-power, ever-ready,
                    radiating.

In the center of this disk
the long-beaked black extended neck
and head of crane. The crane,
all sticks and flaps and wings,
perhaps the "bête" from La Fontaine
who is "méchant," because
"quand on l'attaque, il se défend."
Defends home to the death;
called a vicious nuisance for it.

Radiating, too, like acid-leak:

Painted on this disk, longing, hideous,
an image of the Evil One's ancient face
mid-shriek. The power here is awful,
worse by far than even Rottenbelly's.
Did you think the sacred was all roses?
Take a look at your own face.

> *Invisible wires charge the shields.*
> *Track their snakiness to*
> *the power-pack nearby. Here*
> *innocuous, swaddled carefully,*
> *the Sacred Pipe.*

> They say . . . long ago . . .

Maybe came from Minnesota;
or heaven, maybe, I dunno
brought to us two-leggeds by Woopé
that White Buffalo Calf Woman
who is powerful, who is beautiful
as, as, well, something
like your covergirl —
except she's sacred too

> As legendary Rome at dawn
> Jerusalem at dusk

White Buffalo Calf Woman
taught how to use the Pipe
seven sacred smoking rites

like a city planning map which
outlines: You live here: This is
how: Harmony will follow,

and first lit the American heart
and first burned
inside its bowl of soft red stone
an earth-sky covenant as
bindful as the Ten Commandments or
the Golden Rule, but
American; as this earth
this pipe-bowl, this catlinite:

All Are Relatives.

Some say you know
it is so powerful, a
.50 caliber Minié ball—well
sort of like that Carlton's slider—
just breaks down sharply
and will whiz away
from a properly charged shield . . .
oh those shields, they were . . .
something . . . in the old days, you
know? Powerful. Powerful.

Between pipe and medicine emblem
on the buffalo hide disk, you
yourself, arms stretched out
must complete the circuit, crying
for a vision. But it's not to

yammer on about. You'll do it
if you do it.

        Thus, the rack of batteries,
        the great shields at night;
        at peace behind trademarks —
        but not asleep . . .

Now, night is peeled back.
                East, a stripe
of tangerine. Midnight-blue curtains
rise. Enter the Village Crier,
the morning paper on two legs.
We see him trot among tipis,
dogs, cooking fires, drying strips
of meat on frames. He keeps headlines
big and simple. The warshields jump,

                snatched up! Men jump.
                Mounted. Painted.
                Stripped for quickness.
                Shields — unsheathed — thus!
                Turned around, this way,
                that. Arms
                thrust into straps,
                rotated like ignition keys.

Panting, bent-backed dogs blink,
their pink tongues loll in and out.
Women's eyes dart all sides alarmed —
The kids? Where are the —
Children in the crook of arms
turn this way, that; pudgy fingers

reach to tap an adult nose — stop.
Sense fear. Grandma's neck vein
beats.

A horned buffalo warhelmet
appears among the mounted heads.
Like a magnet, draws eagle-feather
bonnets after, disappears.

Dodging hooves
the Village Crier
holds up the headline
with both arms,
supported by a column
of voice. It says:

Soldiers.

4

On the Rosebud,
June 17, 1876

They come.

See there.

They come.

See there.

From the Southwest now they come,
Colonel Gibbons, General Crook, who
will fight.

Their columns, blue insects
— see? —
file up and down the hills.

Battle pennants
like antennae wave.

Huncpapas watch.
A horse nation sees.

Still they come.

Oglalas watch.
A horse nation sees.

Still they come.

Minneconjou watch. Iron
Thunder points; others nod.
Brulé, Téton, Sans Arc watch.

A horse nation sees.
Still they come.

Sitting Bull flicks
glance at Gall. A Huncpapa
wedge of horse erupts.
Led by Gall, surges left
of the Oglalas. Halts.

The insect files grow.

Cheyenne watch. Wooden Leg
squints, wheels to Dull Knife.
Dull Knife glances to Two Moon.
Eagle plumes shake, waiting.

Insects growing.
Into men. Mustachioed faces,

white. Tunics blue.
Red/white battle pennants
like antennae wave.

A breeze snaps one.

And so they come. Zoom into this:

Crook to Gibbons: " . . . reconnaissance . . .
skirmish maybe, but . . . General Terry . . .
and the Seventh, Custer . . . Reno . . .
you know . . . join us . . . few days . . ."
The wind breaks his speech up
to a Braque still-life
". . . arrive . . . we'll engage — "
Salutes exchanged. Gibbons goes.

And still they come.

> Tashunka Witko
> watching. Eyes
> black. Wolverines
> through white bars.
> The Oglalas wait.

And still.

> Warbonnets across the ridge
> sift the wind for news,
> Eagle plumes bend left
> then right.

And:

> Rain in the Face slips right
> wrist through warclub's
> thong. Hefts it. His pony
> snorts, whips head left, up,
> jerks hooves, listens:

Distant singing, strange tunes.

> Tashunka Witko
> ·vatching; then — not —
> The horned buffalo warhelmet arcs left,
> nods. Hand up, lance up —
> and they move, his Oglalas —
> thus he slips them
> into first, his Oglalas,
> lets clutch out,
> begins to roll.

> Two Moon guns it, this
> splendid shiny red
> 300 horsepower Cheyenne
> Special,
> he just guns it —
> no muffler on this one —
> the warcry from 800 throats
> redlines 6000 rpms
> then —
> the raised lance — that's it!
> pops the clutch —
> a rifle shot —

They go. They peel out
along two long lines of purest shrieks
parallel
racing
lances doubled, shafts beside shafts.

Crook, appalled,
halts, howls:
Troop deploy!
Fears: too late.

Sabers naked,
rifles waving,
a military porcupine
pissing powdersmoke
everywhere;

Horses roiling,
wild-eyed —
deployment's hard.

As in the dream, Tashunka Witko
splits the warrior dignitaries
left and right —

Crook: They're running!
Charge them! Charge!

Seen from above: the locusts, roiling,
form and charge.

A clumsy ocher crab stops to receive
them, spreads claws wide —

> *Now*, Tashunka Witko waves,
> as the spirits whisper to his arm,
> horned buffalo warhelmet nods,
> Gall there, Hump there, Two Moon —

> Draw back draw back
> let them come

Let them? Disgruntled Lakota heads, grim. *Is this
our way to — ?*

> Draw back draw back, *let them come*
> draw back draw back —

Warlances, rifles, warriors like a field of grass
the wind scythes left in sheaves, then right,
widening a path.

> Circle wide now — wide! —
> legs, ligaments at full stretch
> lips, eyelids at full stretch
> Ponies screaming swerve
> wild-eyed, left and right —

> Now — in — *pincer! Pincer! Pincer!*

> And holds the center with Two Moon
> while at the flanks

Gall and Hump race in
unstoppable today
and in forever's memory,

their impact such
contemporary men still stroll
around the craters where they hit
and do not imagine that they aged
or drank or sickened, or despaired,
their medicine failed, or faith
grew feeble, or their surviving
children's glow went snuff
on reservation rations; or
that they died.

                    Crook's flanks cave in
                    like geriatric hips.

Crook must: "Pull back!"

                    And does.

                    •   •   •

                    You can hear the river on its rocks
                    again. You can . . . if you so wish
                    draw in the breath of pines.
                    Imagine: this sweet momentary
                    stillness: how it heals this
                    landscape — as if that cloud
                    of European noisesomeness
                    which rolled 100 feet high west
                    from Jamestown and from Plymouth
                    had folded back reluctantly
                    upon itself
                    into
                    the Atlantic.

They're gone.

Spilled, a
box of wooden matches
on a hill, the dead.
Eyes hooded, empty
buckets.

These boys grew up with dreams
to kill an Indian and be men.
Perhaps some did. I hear
wailing here and there.
Grieving arms are being
slashed with knives. Perhaps . . .

. . .

Night
Fires pour sparks up-
wards.

Is the rhythm distant?
Come closer in. See
the drummer's hands
nimble as
the wings of dragonflies.

Paha Sapa   Paha Sapa
Men recite the day's exploits,
and feet stamp in the kill-dance.

And knowing this earth beautiful
pray for men killed today

as honor will oblige them to, till
the beauty is struck off them too.

> Paha Sapa! Paha Sapa!
> Never will we sell them
> never will we sell them
> never what is sacred
> never what is holy,
> whoever tries to take them,
> He will hear my gun!
> Stamp, go feet,
> stamp,
> feet moving in the dance, and

prayer, nose tilted forward
helicopters up — away.

> He will hear my gun!

Cousin to wounded cousin: We have won!

> Excited by the drums, ululation
> rises.
> Fireflies chase sparks
> and mate.

The medicine and the military
tolerate the ecstasy.
But, do not believe it.
Agree: move camp at dawn; one
river west.

5

Custer's Dreams Prefigure Television

Eastward, dreaming,
Custer
not liking dance shows
in a foreign tongue
— Paha Sapa — cha cha cha —
irritable
flicks channels — cha —
hoping for some midnight porn.

Catches General Terry
his commander telling Johnny Carson:

> "Johnny, treaties or no treaties
> we just can't keep goldminers out.
> It isn't fair. The Black Hills
> are simply veined with it."

Johnny's sidekick Ed McMahon:

"Gold, General? My goodness. Really?"

"That's right, Ed, gold; and we
tried negotiations; we tried to buy
those hills. Well basically
the Sioux refused . . . now if we can't
establish forts nearby to protect
our miners — who are men like you and me —
the Indians are going to sit on all
that wealth and — who knows — pray to it."

Ed McMahon:

"Pray? My goodness, really? Do they . . . ?"

Johnny:

"Of course — " quick, sly, "Ed would
know nothing about praying to gold."

The audience roars, Ed applauds,
Johnny cocks head, grins,
breaks for a commercial.

Custer snorts: if they can't establish forts,
no kickbacks from the trading posts
to bring soldiers in on payday.
And a gentleman has expenses
after all. Ergo, civilization equals forts . . .

General Terry drones.
Manifest Destiny

worms out his throat
dances briefly for the folks
becomes a TV personality.
"Treaties or no treaties . . ."
and "must have the Black Hills . . ."
and "sacrifices to be made . . ."
Custer, bored
flicks channels, finds Dreams Express,
his porn. Now dreams all
action without meaning
his steed plunging
on the Greasy Grass
he hurls rivals off his Rosebud
both Crazy Horse and Sitting B.,
and seizes
and squeezes with both hands
and fastens on with eager lips
great mountains like big tits
Grand Tetons!
and dreams — universally
he thinks —
of glory, gold and being adored
despite a certain lack of
morals.

Some dreams, so strong
you must die to wake
from them.

Just so, the homicidal Longhair's.

6

Custer Attended
by Butterflies

June 25, 1876,
in real life too
General Terry drones:
"*Your* scouts?" Gives
up. "What do they say?"

My Crows report a village, Custer says,
a big Indian village
on the Little Big Horn River.

Terry thinks, asks:
"How big, George? . . . "

Well . . . not that big.
You know Indians exaggerate.
I'll see what it's about, he says.
Me, Benteen, and Major Reno.

Terry, hopeless:
"Stick to orders, Colonel,
just for once, will you?"

As well ask stones to flow.
His mind, a child's primer:
A Village Is To Attack.
George is the spoiled boy
who knows the adult-pleasing trick:
attack, whack! turn to Mommy —
smile.

Colonel! From this fool?!
By the end of this campaign
I will have your star upon
my shoulders, Terry-boy
and will never have to listen
to my name and a lesser
rank than yours
come out your trap again!

Born to command all
but his own ferocious vanity,
Custer, livid, wheels his mount
and goes.

God puts a check beside
his name, halfway down the
list. Recommended
watching for the day.

Earth sweats beneath the Smile.
A spider crawls inside the shade
of granite overhangs. It's cool.

.   .   .

Late that day, crows on the wing

as light fades in the powdersmoke
from cerulean to less-deep blue — azure, say —
to powder blue, to deathly grey,
Custer, keeling over on his brother
Tom's dead body, thinks:

So many of them? Darn.

As the terraced cornice of a temple
in a Chinese painted screen
of a battle epic mostly opaqued-out
by gilded clouds is seen,
he briefly glimpses now
the horned buffalo warhelmet
six dark hawk feathers canted back,
the Oglala directing battle traffic,
thinks:

Crazy Horse.
He'll live. I'll rot.

Spaced-out by shock
dying of wounds to lung, groin, liver,
pancreas, neck and head,

seeks balm in celebrities: wonders
which is Two Moon, which is Gall,
where's Hump, Dull Knife, Sitting B.? —
Interrupts himself to denounce Last Stand Haberdashery:

> My tailor will not
> like this spiny look.
> For porcupines, mais oui, on you,
> it is an insult!

But it sticks as certain
insults do, and hurts.

> There is worse: Howl! Chop. Howl! Smash!

Enter finally the Howling Savage
Custer's Mama warned him not to be,
and sent him to play elsewhere.

Chief Gall, the dying man sees; immense
in life, Gall's more immense than life
in grief. Word's come: *Oh Pizi,*
your children — Yes? In the attack — Yes?
All killed! ALL? Gall howls. Kids,
gone, like parents, gone; twice-orphaned
Gall
cries out to the *tunkashilas*
who rule all,
splinters carbine butt golfing some soldier's grimace off,
hurls carbine away followed by twelve sobs,
and thrashes about the toppling men
with studded warclub,
so horrible that Face in Clouds Speaking,

Rain in the Face, Iron Thunder and
Wooden Leg all halt mid-coup to
watch the warchief orphan's grief.

Wooden Leg turns away and vomits.

Gall smashes horrified soldier faces
mirroring his own horrified face
chops living limbs from trunks
threshing men like grass
and dying Custer notes the great Huncpapa's
gimmick as: *Why he has just climbed up*
on his own screaming misery to make
me think he's — oh my god!
he is twelve feet tall. Howl! Gall stumbles
among the dying, howl! Smash! howl! chop!
his arm filthy with man-tissue
Howl! howl! die, die, die, die, die!
Custer's eyes slide shut just as
he sees: a somehow-familiar
female ghost,
a spirit-shaft attached to Gall's
great piston arm
driving it up and down — smash!
up and down, and
pale bits of bone and brain spray up,
the Howl, the ALL? made palpable.

On him now, around him, racing hooves,
bows stretched, thudded bowstrings,
shafts whipping in
whipping in
the American centaurs circle

Sioux Cheyenne Arapaho
amber black and white-streaked
monarch butterflies
on
this blue cornflower.

Butterfly language clarifies.
Lucid! Logical! Inspired as Bach cantatas!
The sprout in him's reborn.
The presidential timber dies.
He understands: *I had no ears.*
Liebster Gott! Wann
werd' ich sterben, the
Redskins knew! All Creation
speaks, if you —

What Creation says
now blotted out by —
Howl! *it comes*
envelops and shakes
his plasm utterly as
his face shatters, implodes to pulp as:

A warlance slanted
downward
from a racing horse
raps his clavicle.
It breaks. There is
a whoop, a Hoka hey!

Someone, he thinks,
counting coup.

Hoofbeats — louder. Thunder!
Another swat.
Another. Cries:

A good day to die!
A good day to die!

He'd have preferred another.

Interlude:
The First Snows

See them,
      ultimatums
            floating down
                  like snow.

From Washington,
      ultimatums
            floating down
                  like snow.

From General of the Armies Sherman
      ultimatums
            floating down like
                  snow.

From General Crook, General Miles
      ultimatums
            floating down
                  like snow.

From General Terry
                    . . . like snow.

Flake by flake
the landscape whited by:

          Come into Fort Robinson and surrender
          or be hunted down like dogs, and die.

Impossible to hunt for winter storage
and to fight.

Prudent as the game,
hard to find these days,
Sitting Bull splits to Canada
a/k/a Grandmother Land,
a kind of government-in-exile, term
five years; head-clearing as exile is
and as full of sorrows and of outbursts
of love for what's been lost
and hate for who has taken it
sharing what is meager fairly
all being meager except sorrows
sharing finally surplus grief
only with those exiled powers equal to its rigor,
the Grizzlies and great Browns
who too
have relatives making rugs
in heartbreaking places.

          Crazy Horse for
          reasons of his own

and that being enough
remains on ground
no one has dislodged
him from
eyes fixed on
        snow
             falling.

      ●   ●   ●

A hunting party story will conclude
this interlude.

In a flurry of slanting white,

        a male deer between two firs,
        branches laden with ice cream,
        swings his coatrack head around.
        He blinks.

His eyes meet Tashunka Witko's.
The eyes of the buck speak thus:

        I have been sent to you. I have
        been charged to say: as I have
        been sent, your death will be.
        No one will count coup on you.
        It will be too late: it will have
        taken four generals, four armies, and
        this pitiless frozen season to
        expose your life — to a friend.
        His name I was not told. I
        am charged to say, as well: At

your last look to the sun
your father, as I do; you
will see their death's face in
His, those you call wasichus. I
have spoken as I was told to.
Brother, I would have rather turned
and fled and lived. It will
be too late for me as well if
you do not pity this messenger.

And Tashunka Witko's eyes:

Brother we have no food. Forgive us.

Behind someone's last cartridge fires off.

The buck looks to the sun,
twists, staggers, lifts
one foreleg to run,
topples,
a dynamited factory
all bricks down at once.

Tashunka Witko's companions smile
gently, but he does not see.

Light fades in the eye
of the messenger
from: I Do Not Accept,
to: I accept.

Their practiced gazes estimate:

Some meat, not much,
for all tonight.

A sharpened bayonet begins
the butchering incisively.

A flock of red birds flying
spurts across an endless white.

7

Nothing Here Is Real,
Little Big Man

Some victories are better fled.

Jump cut to December '76:

> Montana winter
> blares from left to right
> 80 mph
> blows down Sioux pedestrians
> Cheyenne cartwheel through the air,
> deer are lifted up pop-eyed
> slamdunked into black treetrunks.

Then zooms back, right to left.

January, '77:

> Snowflakes bunch and clench like fists
> Snowflakes beat and pound our cheeks

my god, what's made them furious!
What is this, this great white ultimatum,
again, this roundhouse
flung again again
onto this small red bruise of people,
Dear Great Spirit
Wakantanka
Great Mystery
tell
why does it punch out tipis, kids,
what have the guilty done
that the innocent shake and freeze
and do not eat. We do not eat . . .

In heaven this may entertain
where the rules of drama are:
do not make a character you
love too much for you to
torment, savage, finally kill.
We love, and it's instructive
to see them go downhill
affirm their triumphs mean
nothing now, how weak and small
they are. On earth it sucks.

Enough's enough.

February zooms back, left to right.

Some Oglalas, Crazy Horse,
some straggling Cheyenne
huddled in red blankets crossed
by one black stripe

to Fort Robinson, to surrender
finally come.

· · ·

In that summer dream, the clue
Tashunka Witko:

> *Nothing here is real.*
> You knew it would be over.

Captive, tho not thinking captive
you repeat it to your former friend:

> *Nothing here is real*
> *Little Big Man. Can't you*
> *see . . . ?* LBM, impassive
> shiny blue in Army tunic,
> now an Agency policeman.
> *Do you know what this world is?*
> *A shadow, Little Big Man, even*
> *shorter than your own . . .*

Bricklayers at their work
get into this rhythm
mortar, brick and brick and brick
mortar, brick and brick and brick
laying down the perfect lines.

Just so, Tashunka Witko, you
use silence as your bricks,
words as mortar — they dry fast,
and crumble on the tongue . . .

LBM, head down, nods dumbly.
You note his breathing is uneven.
Is strolling at your side an effort?

Two soldiers fall in step behind.
They track your heat, begin to close,
a brace of Phantom F4's homing in.

LBM stops: Seize him.

Each soldier grabs an arm.

What foolishness is this?

Above, Fort Robinson, mist.
A pale wintery sun.
Paradeground empty, save
three figures holding one.

The old stories knew
what misdeeds were primal, what
punishment. They flash at you — oh,
fool Yata gambling heritage away
to malevolent Iktomi! Assassination?
This? Impossible, not from LBM — and yet . . .

And yet
how strange to see him, Little Big Man
wear their coat.
For, he was there this Indian
he was once your very voice
your emissary

hurtling into that treaty council
Fort Laramie Treaty Council
it was Little Big Man galloping in
horse hurdling the impassive Chiefs —
most resigned to loss, some
lemon-lipped, acid-eyed but hopeless
utterly, some avid for the signing gifts,
some just in love with pomp and
their own oratory, but, all —
all — looking up at — LBM! —
yes, the startled U.S. Commissioners too,
who abruptly stood,
beards split by open mouths
as Little Big Man, pistols waving,
shouted at all what you said
quietly enough to him:
THE FIRST MAN TO SELL ONE INCH OF
THESE BLACK HILLS I WILL SHOOT DEAD!
And helped you whip them twice
twice in eight days.

Now? Now helps drag you Tashunka Witko
to the guardhouse
the black irons for wrists and ankles.
No. You snap reminders of your
powers.

        Former brave interrupts with
        his despair: You still believe that
        stuff! I don't! They are locusts,
        they are everywhere!

Ever the child, Little Big Man? Contemptuous
as you can be, Tashunka Witko, to
those in thrall to you who need to
be in thrall to some man or another
as you, visionary, do not need.
Ever in need of shoring up!
What have you been drinking?!
Warrior once, self-propelled hangover now!
Where on the wasichus *do you kiss!*

> LBM, behind you in controlled hysteria:
> It is your fault. They told me that.
> While you live they won't let us be.

While I live, I am Lakota!

A guard shakes you: Whoa there,
> Calm down . . .

And pulls your arms wider. And:
you get it finally: him.

> In a fury twisting round to see behind,
> slipping one wrist loose
> you try to frighten Little Big Man:
> *They can't hold me — look.*

You succeed.

Ex-buddy, someone,
slams the bayonet up your kidney, it splits,

twists through two ribs, breaking one,
splinters fang into a lung.

       Your head, astonished,
       jerks up to the sun.

       Oh. Oh.

It isn't real, you know
Yet . . . feels real
Worse, far worse
than: even love for —
whatshername . . . ?

       Little Big Man draws the grooved
       long steel insult out.
       " . . . warned you . . . " drifts from
       his frightened throat.

You say, "Let me go, my friends . . . You have hurt
me enough . . ."
And turn away, forever.

       The soldiers let him drop.
       On the earth the crumpled Chief
       shrinks violently clawing earth
       seems small somehow somehow frail —
       he sucks air and expels it out — sucks,
       expels — ah this uphill struggle —
       to take in air — he fails —
       face in dirt, spine cantilevered
       humps back up, raises throat — up — up — up —
       sucks at the entire atmosphere — he fails —

not air enough on earth — he shrinks —
this failure to get air enough is
unupholstering him somehow . . . he falls.

The soldiers breathe hard too
kids mesmerized by the cruelty.

Is he trying to speak,
Little Big Man? Is he — ?

This Tashunka Witko always
was a puzzle, even to the
long-nosed shrewd Oglalas.

You lean close just in case.
You or your imagination note
his wound has formed itself
into a pair of bloody lips:

Now you have mugged the other world,
how do you hope to enter it?

A guard, puffing: What's he say?

Little Big Man glances round.
Best carry him somewhere comfortable
to die; and think of explanations
for your friends. Also, best a
messenger to Starchief Miles to
say: It's done.

LBM, a shrug, a guess: Just Indian stuff . . .

They bear the tiny body up
and to its final mysteries.

•   •   •

Draw back from this hallucinatory
close-up to,
say, the Milky Way,
Sirius B if you prefer,
someplace big-horned spiral galaxies
can graze among black meadows
of that clean huge acreage —
see God who takes his duties
to each people seriously
now bolt on snip-snap
the light-years-wide Wakantanka tearducts
and begin to weep.

For Tashunka Witko?
Well I don't know, not
exactly probably, not
per se.

Still . . . His old weakness for great
cavalry commanders! Ah, it is amigos
like those somewhat too long canines.

No one ever mentions it.
And perhaps it's not worth mention.
When all is said and done —
He is He.

Success below
success above
knows once you have it all
people call it all successful
even history —

which He calls
Love.

8

Last Rites

In Washington, Cump Sherman slides
half a dozen Chesapeakes
off their shells right down his throat.
Downs half a dozen more with toasts.
Glasses clash.
Officers pop up and down.
Sherman thinks of slightly sweaty
joggers' breasts in Rock Creek Park.

He's never liked these affairs,
claims he's seen too much,
meaning that which his own hands performed,
to ever celebrate more death —
Still —
Sioux whipped *and* Custer, that pest,
dead. By God. It was
too much to hope for.

Rises. Tries a smile, glares; from
grim lips issues this: Gentlemen!
(All rise) A toast!

.   .   .

In Brooklyn Walt Whitman reads the news,
slides a dozen Bluepoints down
his — oh too bad, Walt — one's bad,
very very very bad.

He cannot contain his multitudes.
American poetry — oops —
throws up.

.   .   .

In the Black Hills, earnest
workmen slam hammers into hillside stone
plant dynamite, plunge plunger-handles down, boom,
puff out four white famous faces
to overlook the victory.

Each day they look down on this:

        steam escapes a sweat-lodge
        medicine of the stones
        squeezed out hissing
        protest, ornery.

        Now one old man emerges
        grey braids plastered on his back.

Was he there that day?
Always there I guess.

He says: *Mitak' oyassin!*

Now another with ironcolored crewcut
his plumber's tools off to one side
jeans jacket slung over them,
gravely: *Mitak' oyassin.*

Emerged they plant feet wide for leverage, facing east,
spread their wrinkled arms, wide, wider,

crewcut trying to remember
braids unable to forget

lift furrowed landscape faces
to the perpendicular
and chant.

Praying for all on earth
that is created and creates
with unfathomable gravity,
they who hold world records
against the Seventh Cavalry —
twice, twice in eight days —
now strain, now
get beneath, now
raise
by vertical degrees
the record-breaking
thermo-mega-
tonnage

                 of —
              together now — snatch, jerk! Hah!
              the blameless sun.

Dawn rises on rusted piles of
auto skeletons.
Also, a scorched whiskey bottle
someone's thrown away.